D1449696

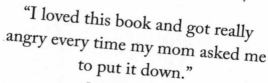

"I loved this book and got really angry every time my mom asked me to put it down."
—Lottie, age 8

"It was an amazing adventure and I especially like the cat, Thunder."
—Rida, age 6

"I loved the meaning of the book—we should all do more to save our world. I can't wait for the next one!"
—Florence, age 7

"I liked Thunder because he is fluffy and he's got one eye and he talks."
—Molly, age 5

Katy

Chatty, sociable, and kind. She's the glue that holds the Playdate Adventure Club together. Likes animals (especially cats), and has big dreams of saving the world one day.

Cassie

Shy but brave when she needs to be. She relies on her friends to give her confidence. Loves dancing, especially street dance, but only in the privacy of her bedroom.

Zia

Loud, confident, and intrepid. She's a born leader but can sometimes get carried away. Likes schoolwork and wants to be a scientist when she's older, just like her mom.

Thunder

Big, white, and fluffy with gray ears, paws, and tail. He's blind in one eye, but that's what makes him extra special. Likes chasing mice, climbing trees, and going on adventures. Is also a cat.

Join Katy, Cassie, and Zia
on more Playdate Adventures

The North Pole Picnic
The Magic Ocean Slide
The Giant Chestnut

THE WISHING STAR ★

★ THE PLAYDATE ★
ADVENTURES

KATY   ZIA   CASSIE

THUNDER

THE WISHING STAR

Emma Beswetherick

Illustrated by Anna Woodbine

ROCK THE BOAT

A Rock the Boat Book

First published by Rock the Boat,
an imprint of Oneworld Publications, 2020

Text copyright © Emma Beswetherick, 2020
Illustration copyright © Anna Woodbine, 2020

The moral right of Emma Beswetherick to be identified as
the Author of this work has been asserted by her in accordance with the
Copyright, Designs, and Patents Act 1988

ISBN 978-1-78607-865-0 (hardback)
ISBN 978-1-78607-965-7 (ebook)

Printed and bound in Great Britain by Clays Ltd, Elcograf S.p.A.

This book is a work of fiction. Names, characters, businesses, organizations,
places and events are either the product of the author's imagination or are used
fictitiously. Any resemblance to actual persons, living or dead, events
or locales is entirely coincidental.

Oneworld Publications
10 Bloomsbury Street, London, WC1B 3SR, England

Stay up to date with the latest books,
special offers, and exclusive content from
Rock the Boat with our newsletter

Sign up on our website
oneworld-publications.com/rtb

MIX
Paper from
responsible sources
FSC® C018072

To Archie and Isla,

for opening my eyes x

CHAPTER ONE

To everyone else it was an ordinary morning on an ordinary Tuesday. Throughout the town, children were waking up, eating breakfast, and getting ready for school without giving much thought to the day ahead. But for Katy, today was anything but ordinary. As she charged from her bedroom—long hair a mess, uniform on crooked, school bag spilling out books, and pens—Katy couldn't decide if she was nervous or excited. She was nervous-cited—that's what she was! Her very new best friends were coming

for their first ever playdate, to her house after school, and now it was almost here she felt just about ready to *pop*!

"Dad, do you think Cassandra and Zia will like coming to our house?" she asked from the kitchen table, as she hurried down spoonfuls of honey-coated cereal.

"Of course! Who wouldn't?!" He smiled.

Katy grinned. She didn't have any brothers and sisters and only lived with her dad, who always had a knack of knowing what to say.

While her dad tugged her dark blonde hair into a high ponytail, Katy brushed her teeth as quickly as she  could get away with. Then she rushed into the hall to put on her school shoes, tripping over an enormous cat lying in the doorway.

"Thunder! Why do you always have to lie

2

in my way?!" she giggled, heaving him into her arms and nuzzling his soft fur. "My friends are going to love you," she continued, as she plopped him down on the floor behind her and blew him a kiss goodbye.

Thunder was Katy's one-eyed rescue cat. He was huge, incredibly fluffy, with a white tummy, a gray face, paws, and tail. Apart from Cassandra and Zia, he was Katy's absolute best friend in the world.

3

"Come *on*, Dad, let's *go!*" she shouted, as she opened the front door and the cold morning air filled the narrow hallway. Katy shivered.

"Coming, coming," Dad laughed as he whipped his coat from the hook and followed his daughter out of the front door.

It's today!, Katy said to herself, feeling butterflies fluttering inside her tummy as she walked to school. Katy was new to her class at Bishop's Park Primary and, as she'd discovered at the start of term, this was not an easy thing to be. All the other girls had groups of friends already, so when Cassandra and Zia had asked her to play with them, she'd wanted to hold on to their friendship as tightly as she could. Now, even though it felt as if she'd known the girls for ever—which is why she felt cartwheels-in-the-air excited about today—she was also just a teensy bit nervous. More than anything, she

wanted desperately for them all to remain the very best of friends.

Over the past few weeks, Katy, Cassandra and Zia had formed their own special club, called the Playdate Adventure Club. They'd been learning about Earth at school and their teacher, Ms. Coco, had talked to the class about all the amazing places in the world. She'd told them about the rainforests in Brazil and the frozen Arctic, a mountain called Everest and the Sahara Desert. Every playtime they pretended to go on a new adventure and after school they planned to have their biggest adventure yet.

"We could go on safari in Africa, with lots of wild animals!" exclaimed Zia.

"How wild?" asked Cassandra, fiddling nervously with her Afro. Cassandra's curls were legendary in class for the giant array of bows

5

and clips and hairbands she wore each day, often all at the same time.

"Really wild!" Zia laughed, but Cassandra didn't look so sure.

"Don't worry, Cassie," said Katy, putting her arm around her friend's shoulder. "We'll only go on adventures we all want to go on."

Cassandra looked happy with that as the bell rang and they lined up outside Junipers' classroom, ready for afternoon class.

Throughout the rest of the school day, Katy tried her hardest to concentrate, but she couldn't stop thinking about all the cool things she could play with her friends that afternoon.

"Katy, are you with us?" asked Ms. Coco.

Katy realized the whole class was looking her way.

"Um, sorry, Ms. Coco. Can you repeat the question?" She could feel her cheeks turning pink as she spoke.

"I asked if you could remember which planet comes after Earth in the solar system?"

"It's Mars. The red planet!"

Ms. Coco nodded and carried on talking, but once again Katy's thoughts started to wander. Of course she knew which planet came after Earth. She also knew which planet came before, and the one that came after the one after. In fact, Katy knew the order of *all* the planets in the solar system, because she'd made a model with her dad last weekend and brought it in for show-and-tell. Perhaps they could have a space-themed playdate today? Yes, her friends would love that. She tried to

7

get Zia and Cassandra's attention, but Zia was concentrating on the lesson as usual while Cassandra was doodling in her workbook. And anyway, Katy didn't want to get into any more trouble with the teacher. It would have to wait. Oh, if only the lesson would *end*!

Finally, at 3:15p.m., the bell went and the girls erupted out of the classroom in a flurry of coats and book bags. Zia's braid—which Ms. Coco said reminded her of a giant black python—knocked their space pictures off the windowsill in her rush to get to the door first.

"Oops! Sorry, Ms. Coco!" Zia giggled.

"No problemo!" Their teacher waved theatrically.

Then Katy saw her dad waiting outside, and they all ran toward him in a mass of laughter and hugs.

"PLAYDATE, PLAYDATE, LET'S GO ON A PLAYDATE!" they chanted.

But what Katy, Cassandra and Zia didn't realize as they wove their way out of the school gates, falling over scooters and strollers in their eagerness to leave the playground, was that something incredible was about to happen at Katy's house.

Because Katy had been right that morning.

This really was no *ordinary* Tuesday.

CHAPTER TWO

Katy's home was only a short walk from school and the three girls held hands all the way to the front door. She lived on the upstairs floor of a small but pretty, thin sort of house, painted buttercup yellow and nestled in between two taller houses each side.

As soon as her dad opened the door, Katy charged straight up the stairs and through to the den, calling to her friends to follow as they left a trail of coats, shoes, and bags strewn across the hallway.

"Zia, Cassie, meet Thunder," she said, as the

gray and white fluffy cat jumped off the couch and began to slink along the carpet, rubbing itself against Cassandra's legs and depositing a dusting of fur on her school pants.

"He's cute," said Zia.

"*So* cute. But what's wrong with his eye?" asked Cassandra, stroking him with one hand while picking white hair off her legs with another.

"Before my dad rescued him, he got into a fight with another cat. He's now blind in one eye." Katy gazed at her pet proudly. "But the other eye works fine. My dad says it makes him extra special, and makes looking after him extra-specially important."

"He's very friendly," Cassandra said, as Thunder started purring like a tractor. "And very loud!"

The girls burst out laughing while Zia and Cassandra began to look around the room, eyeing up the unfamiliar toys. Katy had boxes of toys and games stacked neatly along the back wall, under the window.

"Right, what shall we do first?" asked Zia, taking control as usual.

"We could play with your Legos?" suggested Cassandra, noticing a large container of bricks in the corner.

"We *could* play Lego," Katy said thoughtfully. "But I had an idea in class today. You'll have to come to my room to see what I mean though. Come on."

Katy raced out of the den and across the small landing into her bedroom, jostling her friends inside and shutting the door.

"Welcome to my room!" She flicked on the light switch—it was already getting dark outside.

13

Zia and Cassandra's eyes soon settled on the constellation of stars on Katy's bedroom ceiling.

"Wow! That's so cool! Did you stick them up there yourself?" Zia asked.

"Yes, but my dad helped me. Just wait until you see how they glow in the dark. Watch!"

Katy pulled her curtains closed and flicked the light switch off again, then gazed in delight at the ceiling. Above them, the sky was aglow with yellow and purple and pink and blue fluorescent starlight, starry patterns zigzagging their brilliant way across the room.

"Amazing!" said Cassandra, gazing upwards in awe. "My big brother has some on his ceiling too, but they're no way near as cool as yours."

"Thanks, Cassie." Katy smiled. "I love them so much, especially that huge yellow one at the end. Dad calls that one the Wishing Star. He says that if you really want something hard enough, you need to visit the Wishing Star and make a wish. But it's really difficult to get there. And that's why not many wishes actually come true."

"Do you think your dad's right?" asked Cassandra. "I'd love my wishes to come true."

"I'm not sure," answered Katy. "But that's what I was wondering about at school today when Ms. Coco was talking about space. Do you think today's adventure could be to the Wishing Star?"

Everyone thought for a second.

"Yes!" Zia enthused. "I've always wanted to see what Earth looks like from space. And we could all think of a wish before we get there!"

The two girls looked at Cassandra, who was still staring up at the ceiling, until finally her freckly nose unwrinkled itself. "I think we should do it!" she agreed, and Katy and Zia started jumping up and down.

"An adventure to the Wishing Star. That's perfect!" beamed Zia.

Cassandra spun around and punched the air in a new move she'd been practicing in her street dance class—she was always trying out her new moves.

"Nice move, Cassie!" laughed Katy. "Just one thing though before we get going—we need to figure out a way to get there. Any ideas?"

Just then, they heard a soft scratching at the door, and when Katy opened it, Thunder

sauntered into the room with a foil cup in his mouth and dropped it by Katy's feet.

"Thunder, not now," she laughed, grinning apologetically at her friends. "Thunder's more like a dog-cat than a cat-cat. He likes to bring you things to play with."

She picked up the foil cup and threw it across the room. Thunder pounced on it as though it was a living animal and started pushing it along the floor with his gray paws.

"Dad's going to be mad again. Thunder's always dragging things out of the recycling box."

"Hey, perhaps that's it!" said Zia. "We could make a rocket out of old junk. To get to the Wishing Star, I mean."

"Thunder, you're a genius!" Katy crouched and rubbed Thunder along his back while he wound his way around her ankles, purring

17

loudly. "Wait here," she said firmly, turning back to her friends. "I need to get something important." Then she darted out of the room.

CHAPTER THREE

Katy ran into the kitchen, where her dad was stirring a saucepan of something delicious-smelling on the stove.

"Dinner in about thirty minutes?" he asked, as Katy heaved a box of recycling into her arms.

"Um, yes, sounds good," she replied as she struggled out of the kitchen and back through her bedroom door. She then opened a cupboard to take out scissors, sticky tape and glue, followed by another big box saying *Katy's Craft Box* in bold letters across the top. "OK, I think we have everything we need."

Cassandra stared approvingly at all the boxes, cartons, bottles, newspapers, foil trays, plastic containers and yogurt pots laid out on the floor. "You've got so much stuff!"

Zia started rummaging through all the materials, arranging everything into place on the carpet. "How about we use the biggest box for the command module and cockpit? Then a couple of bottles and some tinfoil for the fuel tanks and boosters. Then we can use scissors to cut holes for the windows... Something like this," she said, drawing frantically on the back of an old envelope.

"*Woah*, Zia! You seem to know a lot about rockets!" exclaimed Katy with wide, green eyes. Then she crouched down to pick up a reel of tape so she could help stick the bottles to the back of the cardboard box.

"I just know a lot about making things!"

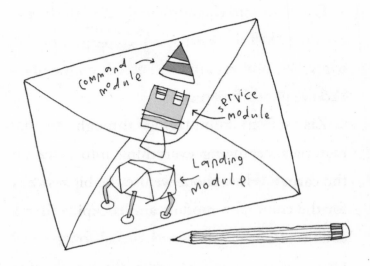

She started digging through more bits of card. "My mom's a scientist and we're always making things at home. Hmm, I'm sure I saw something that would be great for the landing module."

"Is this what you're looking for?" Cassandra picked up a foil tray and passed it to Zia.

"No, but that would make a great TV screen!" Zia laughed.

The girls carried on
working on the rocket
while Thunder lay
curled in the corner,
meowing every now and again in anticipation.
Zia took charge—she always took charge—
but Katy didn't mind, as she knew what a
good leader Zia was. It's what Katy loved
about her new friends—how different they
were, and what a great team they made. Zia
was confident and liked being leader and
Cassandra was shy but *always* sensible. Katy
was the kind and chatty one, apparently, which
pleased her a lot.

After about twenty minutes of the kind of
teamwork that would make Ms. Coco proud,
they put the finishing touches to their spaceship,
then all stood back and smiled.

"Wow, that looks *amazing!*" Cassandra

beamed, her freckles dancing around on her face.

"It does, doesn't it?" squealed Katy.

The hatch at the front of the rocket was just about big enough for the three girls to squeeze through. They'd covered the outside in silver glitter, and inside they'd used old bottle tops and candy wrappers for the control center. The plastic bottles stuck to the bottom, also covered in glitter, looked like real boosters and they'd even managed to find some clear plastic to stick behind the cut-out window. Katy wasn't sure if it was enough to *really* get them to the Wishing Star, but they'd tried their best. And it looked *fantastic*!

"OK, who's ready to go to the stars?" But then she thought a bit more, one finger pressed to her lips. "Actually, I think we need to come up with some kind of code—to mark

our first real adventure."

"You mean like a password to a secret club?" asked Cassandra excitedly.

"Our *Playdate Adventure Club*," corrected Zia.

Katy nodded. "Yes, sort of. Like something we say whenever we want to make the game we're playing turn into something real."

"I like that idea," said Cassandra. "Perhaps we should all hold hands first?"

"And close our eyes?" suggested Zia.

Katy nodded. "And then we need to imagine ourselves getting into our rocket and flying into space. Visualize a huge black space *filled* with glittering stars, with one enormous star ruling the sky! Ready?"

"READY!"

All three girls got into position, grabbed each other's hands and squeezed their eyes as

tightly shut as was humanly possible.

"Everyone say together: I wish to go on an adventure," said Katy.

"*I wish to go on an adventure*," the girls sang out.

To begin with, nothing happened, but after a few seconds, the girls experienced a feeling they'd never, ever experienced before. It was a kind of warm but shivery, fizzy sort of a feeling, like the bubbles in a glass of lemonade were shooting all over the inside of their bodies. They couldn't believe what was happening.

After about ten seconds they started to feel normal again.

"Zia, Cassie, I think you'd better open your eyes!"

CHAPTER FOUR

"*Oh...*" gasped Cassandra.

"*My...*" cried Zia.

"*Goodness!*" shouted Katy.

They were no longer standing in Katy's bedroom, but on the launch pad of a real space station. And when Katy looked at her friends, they weren't wearing their school uniform but were now dressed in white-padded spacesuits with *PLAYDATE ADVENTURE CLUB: STAR MISSION* printed on an orange badge on their left shoulders. They were holding space helmets under their arms, and on their

feet were heavy white boots. And, perhaps best of all, in front of them wasn't the junk-model rocket they'd just spent ages building, but a shiny, new, girl-sized spaceship!

"I can't believe this is actually happening!" cried Katy.

"So we're really going on an adventure?" said Cassandra nervously.

"It looks like we are." Katy smiled.

"Who wants to check out our ship?" asked Zia, racing over to the wide-open, shiny white door, only moments ahead of Katy.

But when they both turned, they could see Cassandra lagging behind.

"Cassie, are you OK?" asked Katy.

"Not really." Cassandra's honey-colored eyes were fixed firmly on the floor. "How are we supposed to know how to fly that thing?" she mumbled.

28

Katy walked back to her friend and put her arms around her, while Zia smiled encouragingly from the doorway. "We understand, Cassie. But we don't have to know—we can figure this out together. Anyway, we *need* you!"

"Yeah, come on, Cassie," Zia said as she walked back over to join them. "Remember that time you didn't want to dance in front of the class, but then you did, and you felt great after? This is going to be the same!"

"And that time at school," said Katy, joining in, "when you had to speak in assembly and you thought you were going to be sick? How great did you feel afterwards when everyone started clapping?"

"O-*K*, I know you're right," said Cassandra. "And I suppose if I have you two with me… But you *absolutely*, *definitely* think we can do it?"

Katy and Zia put their arms around their

friend's shoulders and soon the three girls were standing in a friendship hug.

"We promise," said Katy. "Cross our hearts."

"Hope to die," said Zia, grinning. "Stick a needle in my eye."

"Put a cupcake on your tie? OK, let's go." Cassandra nodded.

Like real astronauts on the TV, this time all three girls walked toward the rocket with their heads held high until they'd climbed the ramp and ducked their heads through the doorway. The door closed automatically behind them.

"So what now?" asked Cassandra.

Katy's eyes moved slowly across the rocket and her insides felt tingly with excitement. The walls and floor and ceiling were the cleanest and sparkliest of whites, with not a speck of dirt to be seen. There was a little round window on one side and at the front were three padded

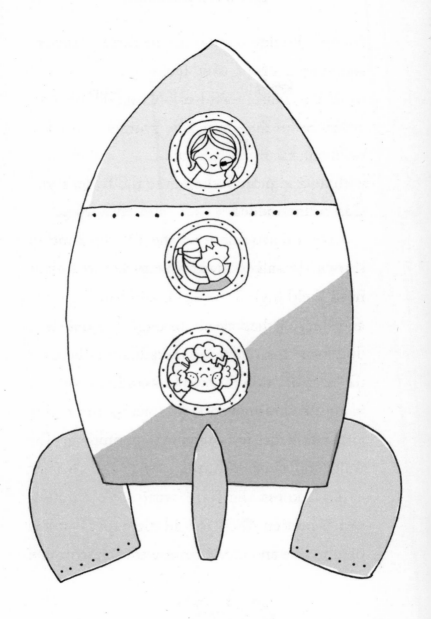

seats with complex-looking buckle systems—
one seat in front of a techy-looking control
panel flashing different colored lights, and two
others behind it, sitting side by side.

"I call pilot!" Zia's large brown eyes flashed
with anticipation as she ran to the front of the
ship before the other two could say a word.

Katy and Cassandra looked at each other
knowingly and took their seats in the second
row.

"Everyone strapped in tight?" asked Zia,
fiddling with the end of her braid while studying
the control panel. Katy could see there were *so
many* buttons in every shape and size!

"I guess so," said Cassandra quietly.

"*Check!*" shouted Katy.

Zia spotted the star-shaped yellow button
which said *BLAST OFF* in big capital letters.
"Are we ready? Everyone, count back with me:

ten, nine, eight, seven, six..."

Meow! The countdown was interrupted by a sound coming from somewhere behind them.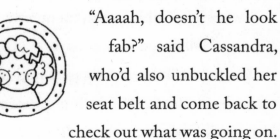

Katy unbuckled her seat belt quickly and turned to see Thunder staring at her grumpily from the back of the ship.

"*Thunder, look at you!*" she screamed. As if it wasn't incredible enough that her room had transformed into a whizzy space station, now Thunder was dressed in his very own spacesuit, with four paw-sized boots and a little dome-shaped helmet fitted snugly over his head.

"Aaaah, doesn't he look fab?" said Cassandra, who'd also unbuckled her seat belt and come back to check out what was going on.

"Does that mean he's coming with us?"

"I think so," Katy replied, "if it's safe to take an animal into space?"

"Actually, the first animal to be launched into space was a dog, so Thunder should be fine!" Zia shouted over to them.

"You always know so much stuff, Zia," said Katy gratefully.

Her friend looked pleased, then went back to studying the control panel.

"OK, Thunder, you can sit with me." Katy had always known Thunder was a special cat, but her dad was right—this proved that he really was extra special. She sat back down in her seat and pulled the safety strap tight across Thunder's tummy—he was now nestling his big bottom into her lap to get comfortable.

34

"Everyone sitting back down?" Zia asked eagerly. "I'm going to count down and press the button for real this time. Ready? *Ten, nine, eight, seven, six, five, four, three, two, one...*"

Katy closed her eyes and squeezed her fists tightly.

"*Blaaaaaast ooooooooff!*"

CHAPTER FIVE

Katy kept her eyes pressed shut and didn't dare move even a muscle. Her arms were wound tightly around Thunder in her lap and her head was pushed against the headrest behind her, her ponytail digging into her helmet. And then, very slowly, she felt the ground begin to move as the rocket lifted off the floor. The roar got even louder as the boosters kicked in and suddenly they were shooting up, up, up into the sky.

ZOOOOOOOOOOOOOOOOOOOOOOOOOOOOOOOOOOOOOOOOOOOM!

"Is…everyone…OK?" she tried to say after what seemed like a lifetime, but the force against her body meant she was finding it difficult to move her lips. And then, finally, after feeling pinned to her seat *for ever*, everything slowed, the roar disappeared, and she started to feel light and floaty.

"That was *wild*!" Zia unclipped her belt buckle and began to remove her space suit and helmet before securing them to a special storage place next to her seat. "Everyone OK?"

Katy glanced sideways and saw that Cassandra looked startled, but when she turned back to look at Zia she gasped. "Zia, what's happening to you?"

Zia was rising up from her seat and floating toward the ceiling like a lost helium balloon.

"I'm floating!" she squealed. "Guys, you have to try this!"

Katy had always wondered what zero gravity felt like. She unfastened her seat belt carefully and pulled Thunder into her arms. "Thunder, are you ready?" she whispered into his ear while also removing her space suit and helmet, and seconds later they were both bobbing around on the ship's ceiling like empty bottles at sea.

"Look, watch this!" Zia pretended to swim through the air and Katy laughed, but when she looked down she could see Cassandra still buckled into her chair.

"Cassie, come and join us!"

"Give me a second, OK?"

Katy saw that her friend's face had turned a bit green.

"We'll be right here," she shouted back encouragingly.

Moments later, Cassandra floated up to join

them, her dancing freckles once more lighting up her face.

"You're right. *This…is…amazing!*" she yelled.

Even Thunder grinned through his helmet as Katy let him drift out of her arms.

Soon the four astronauts were doing their own special floating gymnastics on the ceiling—somersaults and cartwheels and backward rolls and handstands (and street dance moves)—laughing and giggling (and meowing) in delight as they adjusted to their weightlessness. Eventually, Katy pulled everyone together, hands held in a tight circle with Thunder in the middle, and legs spread out at the back like a floating star.

"We could do this all day," she said, smiling at her friends, "but if we're going to get to the Wishing Star, we should probably start planning."

"Any thoughts?" asked Zia.

"Not me," said Cassandra, then she looked at Katy. "Did your dad give you any clues?"

Katy thought for a moment. "On my ceiling, the Wishing Star—the big yellow star—is at the final point of a kind of W made up of smaller yellow stars. *Maybe* it's a constellation. Maybe if we look outside…"

Zia floated over to the window and stared out into the darkness.

"Girls, you've got to come and see this," she said.

They took it in turns—the window was only small—but what Katy saw was beyond even her wildest dreams. The sky itself was blacker than ink—darker than she'd ever seen in her life—but was also aglow with millions of stars twinkling like the brightest of diamonds, setting the sky alight in a kaleidoscope of colors.

It was what Katy imagined magic might look like. But there were also five golden-yellow stars twinkling brighter than any of the others, and if you joined them together like a dot-to-dot, they formed the letter W, with the biggest, brightest, and most golden star of them all lighting up the fifth and final point of the letter.

The Wishing Star.

"There it is!" shrieked Cassandra.

"Can you get us there, Zia?" encouraged Katy.

Zia didn't need to be asked—she was already back at the control panel.

But just as Katy turned from the window, she noticed something small was following them. Surely it couldn't be another rocket? This was *their* adventure, no one else's—wasn't it? It was definitely moving closer though, and it definitely wasn't a shooting star.

"Girls, it looks like we've got company," she said nervously, as the dot outside grew bigger. "If we're going to get to the Wishing Star, I think we need to go. *Now!*"

CHAPTER SIX

Strapped back in her seat, with Thunder once more settled on her lap, Katy waited patiently for the rocket to start moving. She waited, and then waited some more.

"Zia, why aren't we *moving*?" she added anxiously.

"Sorry, I'm trying to work out which direction we need to go in."

Katy could see the enormous control panel flashing a multitude of different colored lights, just like the colorful candy wrappers in their pretend rocket at home, but the monitor

screen was still blank.

"You need to turn the monitor *on!*" she urged. "Maybe it works like a GPS. *Maybe* it will show us the way to the Wishing Star."

To the left of the screen was a small *ON* switch, and no sooner had Zia pressed it than the screen came alive with a burst of light. Then the light disappeared and a twinkling letter W  appeared on a black screen, made up of five stars, one at each point of the letter, like an electronic dot-to-dot.

"Press the fifth star, press the fifth star!" Cassandra shouted urgently from her seat.

"Come on, Zia, we have to go!" cried Katy.

"I'm doing it, OK?" said Zia firmly, as she reached over to the screen and tapped star

number five with the tip of her finger.

Instantly, the rocket started moving again, gradually gathering speed as it whizzed its way toward the constellation.

Now they were finally moving, Katy could feel herself relaxing a little, but she still felt nervous about what she'd seen through the window earlier.

"Katy, are you sure you saw another rocket following us?" asked Cassandra after a while.

"I think so. It looked like another rocket anyway," she answered.

"I wonder what they want?" asked Zia.

"Whoever *they* are," said Cassandra.

Everyone was quiet for a moment.

"Have you decided what you want to wish for yet?" asked Zia, breaking the silence. "I can't decide between new roller skates or a karaoke machine!"

"I have!" Cassandra beamed. "I'm going to wish for a new bike. I have to ride my brother's old one and it's still covered in mud and monster stickers. I've *always* wanted a bright, shiny red one with a tinkly bell!"

They all smiled.

"How about you, Katy? What are you going to wish for?" asked Zia.

Katy thought for a moment. Ever since her dad told her the story about the Wishing Star,

she'd been thinking about what her wish might be. A part of her wanted to wish to see her mom again. But she didn't think her friends would understand that wish. She'd also thought about wishing for more adventures like this one, but they seemed to be pretty good at coming up with adventures themselves.

"I'm going to wish for a pony," she said finally. "I've always wanted to ride a horse and I could keep it at the stables by the park. It would be a girl pony called Star and I'd ride her every weekend. Apart from you two, Star would be my best friend in the whole world!"

"MEOW!"

"Except for you as well, Thunder. You'll always be extra special, remember?" Katy continued, rubbing him across his back.

"Wouldn't it be great if Thunder could wish

49

for something too?" Cassandra smiled.

"Cats can't talk, silly," said Zia matter-of-factly.

"Thunder, how about you?" asked Katy, drawing him in for a hug. "If you could wish for anything in the world, I wonder what it would be?"

"A lifetime supply of mice to chase, of course."

Everyone looked wide-eyed with shock. Did Thunder just *talk*?

"Thunder, did you just *say* something?" asked Katy in disbelief.

"I did," replied Thunder, looking pleased with himself.

"But why didn't you tell us you could talk?" Katy questioned.

"You never asked," said Thunder dismissively.

Katy couldn't believe it. This was already the best adventure ever—now she knew she had the absolute *best cat* in the entire universe!

The girls were so busy staring at the talking animal that they failed to notice the loud knocking on the spaceship door.

"Aren't you going to answer it?" asked Thunder, grinning smugly amid all the new attention he was getting.

"What was that?" asked Cassandra, still staring in astonishment.

But Zia was already floating toward the door, frowning.

"Can't you hear that knocking?" she asked, pulling her helmet forcefully down over her thick braid. "Helmets on, everyone! I think we're about to meet *who*ever or *what*ever has been following us."

CHAPTER SEVEN

Taking it in turns to look through the porthole, they let out a collective gasp as a lady with metallic skin, in a shiny gold and silver spacesuit, floated in the doorway, tethered by a long, shimmering rope to a gold and silver rocket stationed only a short distance away.

"Do you think we should let her in?" asked Cassandra.

"She doesn't seem too dangerous," answered Katy. "Zia?"

"I think we need to find out what she wants. OK?"

They all nodded and then used their combined strength to pull a lever that said *UNLOCK* in big capital letters.

The door crept open. They all held their breath, with no clue as to what was about to happen.

Then: "You girls aren't easy to catch!" said the spacewoman, smiling. "I've been trying to reach you ever since you entered our galaxy. No one has reached the Wishing Star constellation before. I'm impressed you're aiming for it!"

Katy blinked a few times to make certain she wasn't seeing things. "But who are you? And why have you been following us?"

"Can I come in?" the woman asked politely. "As much as I enjoy floating around in space, it would be easier to talk inside."

Katy looked at her friends, who were nodding their heads up and down enthusiastically, so

she held out her hand and helped the woman into their ship. When she'd unhooked the rope from her spacesuit and the door was sealed, they removed their helmets and the stranger shook out her long, shimmering gold and silver hair.

"Your hair! I've never seen anything like it before!" cried Katy, wanting to reach out and touch it.

"Thank you," she said, smiling. "I'm Starlet, captain of the Wishing Star Galaxy. We don't get many visitors here. I wondered if you could tell me why you've come?"

Zia moved forward, speaking so quickly she forgot to breathe. "We were on a playdate and thought it could be fun to visit the Wishing Star and we built a spaceship but we didn't know it would actually work but it did and now we're almost there and when we arrive we'd all like

to make a wish and see if it comes true." She took a long breath then swung back toward her friends, catching the spacewoman with the end of her braid as she did so. "Um, sorry!" she said, lowering her head.

"No problemo!" The woman waved theatrically.

Katy couldn't help but think there was something familiar about Starlet.

"So have you all decided what you'd like to wish for?" Starlet then asked.

"We have," they answered in unison, including Thunder, who was now rubbing his soft body against the spacewoman's ankles and winking up at her with his big blue eye.

She crouched down and stroked him softly along his back.

"And may I ask what those wishes are?"

Taking it in turns, they told her exactly what

they'd been discussing only moments earlier. Zia settled on roller skates, because her older sisters already had them and she didn't want to miss out on the fun.

"Hmm," Starlet said with a sigh. "Just as I'd suspected. And that's why I'm here, because before you reach the Wishing Star, I want to show you something important. Please, follow me."

Starlet floated over toward the command module, where she sat at Zia's seat and took a little jar out of her pocket.

"This," she said, "is stardust." She opened the tiny lid and took a handful of glittery powder in her hands. "When I sprinkle it on this screen, it's going to show you a new way of looking at your planet—then you can tell me if you still feel the same about your wishes. Ready?"

The four friends nodded, and with a sweep of

her hand, a glittery cloud filled the air and rained down on the monitor in front of them. The screen burst into life.

"That's Earth!" cried Cassandra, who had been silent up until now.

"Yes, but watch closely," said Starlet, as the image on the screen got bigger and bigger as the picture zoomed in closer.

The familiar sight of Earth gradually transformed until they could see all the incredible places they'd been learning about that term at school: rainforests, jungles, deserts, icebergs, mountains, islands, beaches, rivers, oceans—all the places they'd planned to have adventures to one day.

"Why are you showing us this?" asked Katy.

"Keep watching," said Starlet with a smile, as the film zoomed in even closer.

Now it showed them the even more familiar sight of roads and cars and lorries and buses and houses and shops and schools and playgrounds and parks.

"Hey, that's our school!" shouted Zia.

"And my house!" cried Katy.

Then the film zoomed in closer still, only what it showed now wasn't so comforting. They saw a pile of litter stacked up behind a wall by their school, chip bags and chocolate wrappers strewn across their local park, drink cartons in gutters, bits of paper and cardboard packaging weaving in and out of the wheels of parked cars.

"I don't like the look of that," Zia said quietly.

"Nor me," whispered Cassandra.

The screen changed one last time, making Katy feel sick to her stomach. Images flashed onto the screen, for a few seconds each time, showing a river choking on plastic, forests being chopped down, ice caps melting, and dirty-looking smoke pumping out of cars and factories…

Katy loved her planet and didn't like what she was seeing either. She also didn't understand why the spacewoman wanted to show it to them.

Then, at last, the screen went black.

CHAPTER EIGHT

"So, what do you think?" Starlet broke the silence.

"That this doesn't have anything to do with cats," said Thunder dismissively.

The girls lowered their heads. Katy felt sad and angry and knew her friends must feel the same, but the horrible things they were shown didn't have anything to do with them either, did they?

"I understand what Thunder's saying, because I don't see what any of this has to do with us either. Or our wishes."

The spacewoman crouched down and pulled Thunder into her arms. "Every creature," she said, scratching the cat behind his ear, "every plant, rock, and drop of water on Earth is precious and needs protection. You can't stop every sad thing from happening, but you *can* put your wishes to good use today."

"But what about my roller skates?" asked Zia sulkily.

"And my new bike?" added Cassandra.

The woman held up her hand. "Remember that only one wish can be granted for each of you, so you need to choose carefully. You could wish for something important to *you*, or you could

wish for something important to the *world*. That's the power of the Wishing Star, because you really do have the power to change the world, you know!"

Katy felt goosebumps creeping over her body. She finally understood what Starlet was trying to say and felt an enormous urge to end their adventure the right way.

"I think wishing for a better world is more important than horse riding," she said slowly so everyone could hear her. "Don't you see? Why wish for roller skates or a new bike when there are *bigger* things to wish for?"

Cassandra took a deep breath. "I think I agree with Katy," she announced quietly.

But Zia was fiddling awkwardly with the end of her braid. "I suppose you're right, even though I really, *really* want a pair of roller skates." Then her dark almond eyes seemed

to grow even bigger in size as she looked past them toward the window. "Hey, look! Look out there!" she shouted.

Katy turned and saw that the light around the window was turning gold.

"We've been so busy talking," Zia continued, moving to look outside, "that we didn't realize we're almost at the Wishing Star. Oh wow, come and see! It's *amazing*! No, it's better than amazing. It's *out of this world*!"

Katy looked at Starlet, who nodded as if to give permission for Katy to follow her friends. She floated over to join them and, when she looked outside, was immediately blinded by the most spectacular golden light.

"I can't believe it," said Cassandra, grabbing Katy's hands in her own and squeezing them tight. "I can't believe we actually made it."

Katy had always wondered what starlight looked like close up, and now she knew. It was shinier, and brighter, and sparklier, and more golden than any light you could ever picture in your mind.

"Is that *really* the Wishing Star?" Katy asked.

"Yes, and it's the most powerful star in our galaxy," Starlet answered.

Katy felt extraordinarily happy that her dad had been telling her the truth. All the time she'd stared at the star on her bedroom ceiling

and imagined what it would be like to see the Wishing Star for real. And now she was here!

"For centuries humans have tried to find their way to this star, but until now no one has made it—and no wishes have ever been granted.

But I've been watching you working together and caring for each other, and because of your teamwork—and the fact that you've thought about each other rather than just yourselves— you've been successful in your mission. And that gives me confidence that you'll also think about others when you make your wishes today. So, are you ready? Are you ready to tell me what you wish for?"

Katy beckoned to Cassandra, Zia and Thunder to cluster together, then she bent her head in closer, whispering quietly as she told them her plan. When they'd each nodded their head in agreement, they turned back to face Starlet.

"We are," they all said.

"OK then. Tell me your wishes."

CHAPTER NINE

The girls held hands tightly and looked Starlet square in the eyes.

"I wish for more things to be recycled." As soon as Katy said it, the Wishing Star flashed and she felt herself filling with warmth. It started at her feet and then moved upwards toward her head, radiating outwards and soaking her body in happiness. She then looked at Thunder and her friends, encouraging them to join in.

"I wish for fewer trees to be chopped down," said Cassandra, who must have experienced the same feelings as Katy because she was

beaming in a way that Katy had never seen and dancing round and round in a circle, just as the Wishing Star flashed again and began to shine even more brightly.

"And I wish for people to stop wasting so much water," said Zia, smiling and hugging her body tight to capture the feeling of goodness that their wishes brought. Once more, the star's brightness increased.

Starlet nodded in approval. "But that's only three wishes. How about you, Thunder? What do you wish for?"

Thunder frowned.

"Come on, I know you're a cat, but right now you have the power to change the world!" she urged.

"OK. First though, are mice endangered?" Thunder grinned mischievously.

"No," they all said.

72

"In that case, I wish to protect endangered animals," he said and, after another flash of light, he shook out his fur before launching himself into Katy's arms.

Everyone laughed.

"What happens now?" asked Katy. "To our wishes, I mean? How do we know if they're going to come true?"

"You'll know," said Starlet, "because you'll feel it. That feeling you all experienced just now? That's the feeling you'll get whenever your wish is being granted somewhere in the world. And remember: if you all pick up just one piece of litter every day, or turn off your taps when you're brushing your teeth, the world you live in will be a cleaner and happier place. Small acts of thoughtfulness can make the *biggest* difference. It's that simple."

Starlet then pulled four tiny jars out of her

pocket. "I also want to give you these gifts, to say thank you for wishing so wisely. A jar of stardust for each of you, to remind you what the Wishing Star has taught you. Keep them safe, and when you go on your next adventures you won't forget what you've learned today."

"Thank you," they said.

"Now, who wants to go home?"

Once again, they formed a circle in the air, legs splayed out weightlessly behind them in a star.

"Repeat after me: *I wish to go home*," said Starlet.

"*I wish to go home*," they echoed.

Katy pictured her bedroom at home, the mess of recycling scattered across her carpet, the junk-model rocket by the window, the glow-in-the-dark stars zigzagging across her ceiling.

At once she started to feel funny again—that bubbly, fizzy feeling she'd felt in her room when their pretend adventure had first come to life. Bolts of electricity were shooting all around her body until gradually she felt it return to normal. Then she opened her eyes.

"Did that really just happen?" asked Zia, blinking as if she didn't believe what she was seeing.

"I, um, I think it did!" replied Cassandra, also looking confused when she saw she was back in her school uniform, no space suit in sight.

Thunder was darting in and out of their legs, meowing and acting far more like his usual cat-like self.

Katy checked her pocket and found something hard and small at the bottom.

"The jar!" she squealed.

Her friends plunged their hands into their

pockets as well and that's when Katy realized what their adventure to the Wishing Star had been all about. It had been a test—to see if they could put the world before themselves. And it looked like they'd passed, because inside Katy's jar was a gold bracelet with a tiny charm in the shape of a star.

"Look! It's beautiful!" she cried, taking it from the jar and slipping it on to her wrist.

"I've got one too!" shrieked Zia.

"And me!" cried Cassandra.

"We need to wear these to remind ourselves." Katy smiled. Then she grabbed her friends' wrists and they held their bracelets together in a silent pledge. "Hold on a minute," she said, looking more closely at her wrist. "I think my bracelet has *two* stars on it."

At that moment Thunder started nudging her ankles and suddenly it made sense.

"Cassie, can you hold this?" Katy asked, slipping the second star from her own bracelet before handing it to Cassandra. Then she bent down and pulled Thunder into her arms. "Thunder, I know you can't talk now, but I think Starlet wanted you to have this," she said, fastening the star on to his collar. "It looks like you're part of the Playdate Adventure Club too!"

Thunder grinned a Cheshire cat grin then pounced from Katy's arms and started parading around the room, tail high in the air, the star glinting proudly from his collar.

The girls all clapped and cheered, until they were interrupted by Katy's dad calling them from the kitchen.

"*Dinner's ready!*"

"*Um, coming!*" Katy called back, frowning again at her friends. "He said dinner was in half

an hour. Surely we've been gone longer than that?"

Zia and Cassandra both shrugged their shoulders.

"Well, I suppose we'd better go and eat. Come on! Who's hungry?"

But before they turned to go, Thunder dropped the same foil cup he'd pulled from the recycling earlier by their feet and stared up at them like an expectant puppy.

"Thunder, we're not building another spaceship, silly," Katy said, picking it up from the carpet.

Then it dawned on her what Thunder meant.

"To saving the world, one small step at a time!" she said, placing the cup slowly and deliberately back inside the recycling box. Then she smiled happily at her friends.

Cassandra followed, also picking up a piece of trash from the floor and popping it in the box. "And to the Playdate Adventure Club!" she said.

"And to our next adventure!" said Zia, scooping up the remaining bits of junk and tossing them on top. "I already have an idea where we could go. But we're going to need some warmer coats!"

THE SKY WAS AGLOW WITH MILLIONS OF STARS
TWINKLING LIKE THE BRIGHTEST OF DIAMONDS,
SETTING IT ALIGHT IN A KALEIDOSCOPE OF COLORS.

How to Plan Your Own
Playdate Adventure

1. Decide where you would like to go on your adventure.
2. Plan how you would get there. Do you need to build anything or imagine yourself in a new land?
3. Imagine what exciting or challenging things might happen on your adventure.
4. Decide if you are going to learn anything from your adventure.
5. Most important of all, remember to have fun!

LITTER

☆ ☆ ☆

Did you know…

It is against the law to drop litter in a public place.

Chewing gum is the worst kind of litter as it sticks around for ever—literally.

Not only is litter bad for the planet, it's also bad for animals! Everyday items such as cans and plastic bottles can be deadly for unsuspecting wildlife and even dogs and cats.

Recycling one soda can could save enough energy to run a fourteen-watt light bulb for twenty hours, a computer for three hours, or a TV for two hours.

Cigarettes are the most littered item on earth, with 4500 billion cigarette butts thrown onto streets across the globe every year.

Plastic waste is particularly harmful to underwater life. There is now so much plastic in the sea that by 2050 the ocean could contain more plastic than fish!

Waste should ideally be reused or recycled. Using materials again helps save the Earth's resources.

If that's not possible, waste should always be put in a trash can.

FURTHER READING:

What a Waste by Jess French

Not for me, please!: I choose to act green
by Maria Godsey

The Adventures of a Plastic Bottle
by Alison Inches

Here We Are: Notes for Living on Planet Earth
by Oliver Jeffers

ACKNOWLEDGEMENTS

Since becoming a mom, one of my favorite things has been watching my children navigate the complex yet essential world of new friendships. Seeing them on playdates with their friends has also opened my eyes to the power of what their imaginations can do. So I'd like to thank my two wonderful children, Archie and Isla, and their cousins and friends, for everything they've taught me about being a child again. I'd also like to thank my brilliant husband Tony for his unwavering support and encouragement. Finally, I'd like to thank our two ragdoll cats, Kitty and Kion, without whom Thunder wouldn't have made it on to the page.

The Playdate Adventures would have remained a collection of stories written purely for the enjoyment of my own two children without the help of some brilliant people in the publishing industry. Caroline Sheldon, my agent, for believing in the idea from the very start; Shadi Doostdar, my publisher, for making my dreams come true; and everyone else at Rock the Boat, for their hard work in turning this series into a reality. Finally, the incredible illustrator Anna Woodbine for bringing my characters so perfectly to life.

Emma Beswetherick is the mother of two young children, and wanted to write exciting, inspirational, and enabling adventure stories to share with her daughter. Emma is a publisher with Little, Brown and lives in south-west London with her family and two ragdoll cats, one of whom was the inspiration for Thunder.

Anna Woodbine is an independent book designer and illustrator based in the hills near Bath. She works on all sorts of book covers from children's to adult's, classics to crime, memoirs to meditation. She takes her tea with a dash of milk (Earl Grey, always), loves the wind in her face, comfortable shoes, and that lovely damp smell after it's rained.

Find her at: thewoodbineworkshop.co.uk

If you loved this story, then you will love:

THE NORTH POLE PICNIC

In their next adventure, the girls come face-to-face with arctic animals and what happens when the North Pole begins to melt.

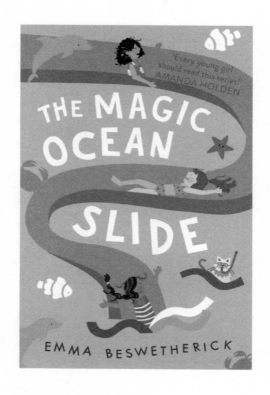

Cover text: 'Every young girl should read this series!' AMANDA HOLDEN

THE MAGIC OCEAN SLIDE

EMMA BESWETHERICK

THE MAGIC OCEAN SLIDE

Katy, Cassie, Zia, and Thunder discover an underwater world and learn there is more to the ocean than meets the eye!

THE GIANT CHESTNUT

Transported into an enchanted forest, the girls
are surprised that the further they go, the fewer
trees there seem to be.

JOIN THE CONVERSATION ONLINE!

Follow us for a behind-the-scenes look
at our books. There'll be news, exclusive
content, and giveaways galore!

You can access learning resources here:
oneworld-publications.com/rtb

Find us on YouTube as Oneworld Publications
or on Facebook
@oneworldpublications